The Usborne Little Children's
SPACE
ACTIVITY BOOK

Rebecca Gilpin

Designed and illustrated by

Erica Harrison

Fred Blunt, Laurent Kling,
Kathryn Selbert, Erica Sirotich
and Dean Gray

Edited by Fiona Watt

You'll find the answers to the
puzzles on pages 61-64.

What's out in Space?

It looks empty, but there are lots of things in Space. There are planets, rocks, storms and stars...

dust, ice and rocks

There are millions and millions of stars. Can you spot six more like this one?

Some planets have rings around them. Colour this planet.

There are huge storms on this planet. Press on the lightning stickers from the sticker pages.

strong winds

Lots of stars move around in pairs. Find all the pairs and draw faces on them.

This is a nebula, where new stars are born. Can you find a way to the star in the middle?

Start here.

huge cloud of gas and dust

Asteroids are big chunks of rock, travelling through Space. See if you can find five more like this one.

3

Astronauts

Put these astronauts in height order, writing 1 next to the shortest one, and 5 next to the tallest.

Who is looking out of the window of the space station?

A

B

C

D

Draw more astronauts on this page.

1. Draw a helmet and a body.

2. Add the arms and legs.

3. Draw a face. Add buttons and stripes.

For a floating astronaut, turn the page before you draw.

Add some stars, too.

Mission Control

It's a busy day at Mission Control.
Can you spot...

- someone pointing at a screen
- a map of the world
- three pencils
- a screen that isn't working
- a clipboard
- two people with headphones

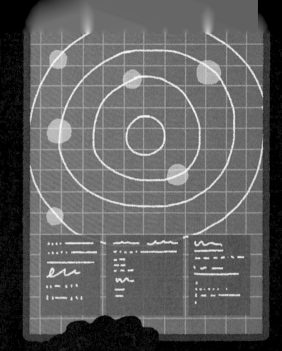

How many mugs
are there altogether? ....

Colour the rest of the lights, following each sequence of colours.

Lots of stars

Stars look tiny and white in the night sky. They're actually giant balls of burning gas far away in Space. And they're not all white...

Look at the stars below. How many of each colour can you spot?

.... blue
(hottest)

.... yellow
(medium hot)

.... red
(least hot, but still incredibly hot...)

Each of these white stars has a brightly coloured twin.
Find each star's twin, then colour it to match.

Look at these views of the night sky. Which one has an extra star?

A   B   C

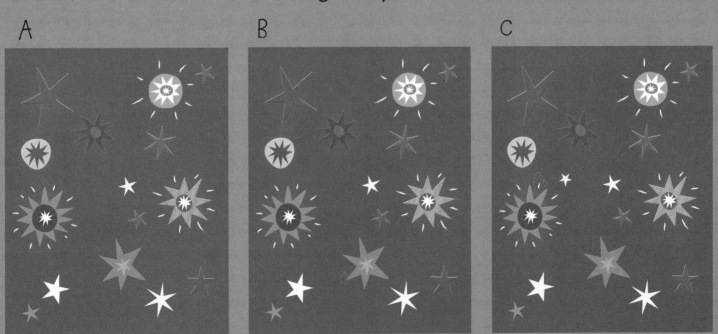

A new world

People are coming to live on this newly discovered planet.
Draw more tracks, then press on stickers from the sticker pages.

a spaceship bringing people

a dome where plants can grow

Press stars and spaceships onto the sky.

a space buggy
transporting
people around

Give the planet a name: ....

Liftoff!

These astronauts are about to board a rocket. Draw smiles on their faces.

It's time for the countdown. Add the missing numbers to launch the rocket.

10... 9... ◯ ... 7... 6...

◯ ... 4... 3... ◯ ... 1...

LIFTOFF!

The rocket has taken off. Draw over the dotted lines to complete the picture.

Back to Earth

A spacecraft is coming back to Earth from a space station.
Which order should the pictures be in? Number them from 1 to 4.

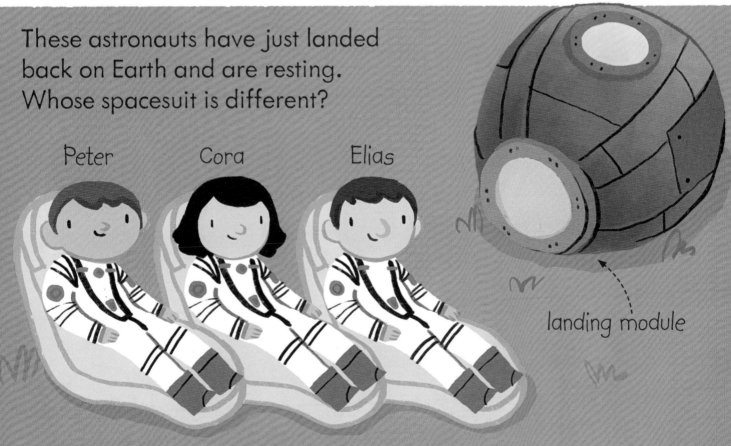

These astronauts have just landed
back on Earth and are resting.
Whose spacesuit is different?

Peter   Cora   Elias

landing module

.........................'s spacesuit is different.

Space colouring

Colour everything on these pages, using pens that match the spots.

Working in Space

Astronauts in a space station have a lot to do.
These three are on a spacewalk, making repairs to the
space station. Which line is each astronaut attached to?

Noah ....   Minna ....   Adam ....

Oops! Someone has let go
of a tool. Can you spot it?

Maisie is doing an experiment, to see how plants grow in Space. Put them in height order, writing 1 next to the shortest one, and 5 next to the tallest.

Astronauts have to stay healthy in Space. They exercise and do tests on themselves. Who has pedalled for longest today?

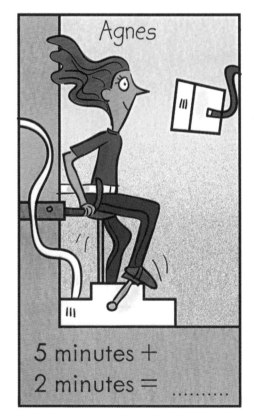

Agnes

5 minutes +
2 minutes = ...

Max

1 minute +
8 minutes = ...

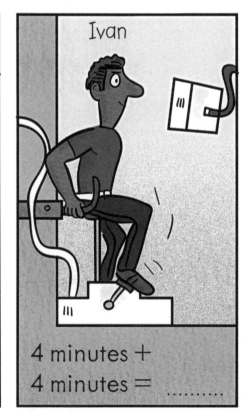

Ivan

4 minutes +
4 minutes = ...

.... has pedalled for longest.

Over 40 years ago, astronauts landed on the Moon.
They explored in a moon buggy, collected rocks and took photos.

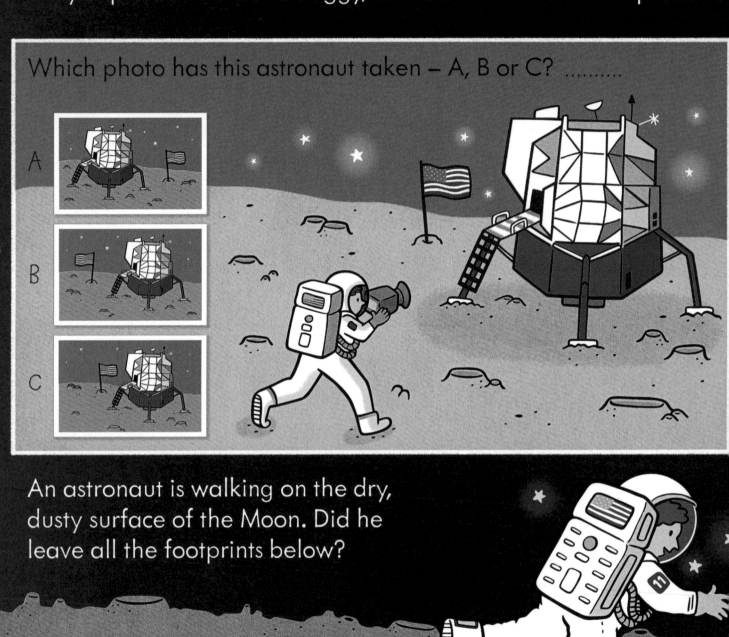

Which photo has this astronaut taken – A, B or C? ....

A

B

C

An astronaut is walking on the dry, dusty surface of the Moon. Did he leave all the footprints below?

YES / NO

The astronauts could see Earth from the Moon. Find the Earth sticker on the sticker pages and press it on.

There are huge craters on the Moon. Draw more craters, like this:

1. Draw an oval.

2. Add lines for the sides.

3. Fill in half of the oval for a shadow.

4. Add rocks near the crater.

Astronaut training

Before people are chosen to be astronauts, they are tested and given training. Ted, Amy and Leo are doing survival training. They must build a camp:

- among trees
- next to water
- nowhere near a bear

Should they build it in site A, B, C or D? ....

A

B

C

D

Ella and Stan have been chosen to train as astronauts.
Can you spot them?

- Ella doesn't have red hair.
- She isn't the smallest.
- She has glasses.

- Stan's top is blue.
- He has dark hair.
- He has black boots.

These astronauts are getting used to wearing spacewalk suits.
Sadie's suit is complete, but four things are missing from Finn's suit.
Can you spot what they are?

Sadie

Finn

21

Draw a rocket...

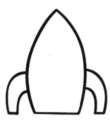  

1. Draw a
pointed shape.
Add two fins.

2. Add a round
window and
rocket boosters.

3. Draw more
details. Colour
the rocket.

Draw more rockets and
planets in this space.

You could add flames
behind a rocket.

...and a planet

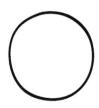

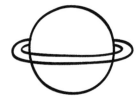

1. Draw a circle or oval for a planet.

2. Add rings around the middle.

3. Draw craters and volcanoes. Colour the planet.

You could draw some stars, too.

Living in Space

This astronaut is packing things to take to a space station. She'll be there for six months. Read the list and look at the picture. Has she got everything? If not, draw what's missing.

a bar of chocolate
two books
a photo of her dog
a pair of socks
a camera
a watch

These astronauts have been in Space for months, and they're thinking about things they miss. Link each pair with a line.

I miss going for a run...

I miss driving my car...

I miss having a bath...

I miss walking my dog...

Everything floats in a space station, so eating can be tricky.
Who is going to eat each pack of food?

Tim is in the space station, talking to his family. Look at the photo
and the computer screen. Who is missing from the screen?
Draw around them in the photo.

Spacecraft

Join the dots from 1 to 10 to complete this spacecraft.

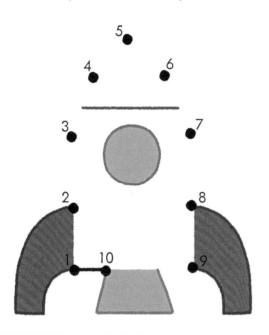

Colour the spacecraft so that the bottom one matches the top one.

Two spacecraft need to meet at a space station. Which way does each one need to go?

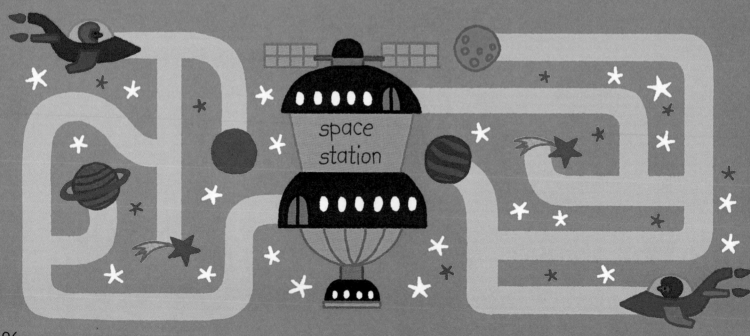

space station

Which spacecraft
is the odd one out?

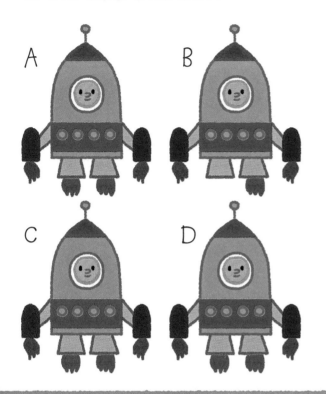

A   B

C   D

Draw a line taking this spacecraft
to each planet, from 1 to 5.

Fill this space with spacecraft stickers from the sticker pages.

Alien party

Can you spot and colour...

...two aliens with spots?

...an alien with three eyes?

...a baby alien?

...an alien with lots of arms?

...seven party hats?

...two aliens dancing together?

Then, colour the rest of the picture.

The night sky

Eric and Lena are looking at the night sky and trying to spot everything in their Space book. Can they see everything?

YES / NO

Which square will complete this night-time scene?

A

B

C

D

Most of the stars below have five points. Can you find two with seven points?

How many stars can Martha see?

....

Dress an astronaut

Using the stickers on the sticker pages, dress these astronauts.

Give them helmets,
spacesuits, gloves
and boots.

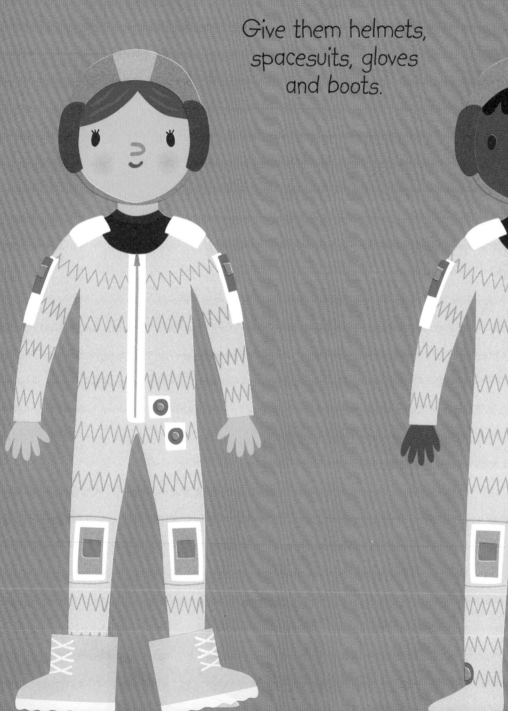

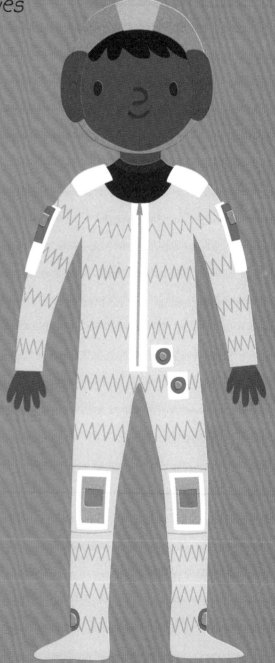

What's out in Space?

Pages 2-3

A new world

Pages 10-11

Visiting the Moon

Pages 18-19

Spacecraft Pages 26-27

Dress an astronaut Page 32

Build an alien　　Page 33

Space tourists　　Pages 38-39

The Solar System　　Pages 42-43

A base in Space   Pages 54-55

There may be too
many stickers here
to fit on your page.

Moon and stars

Page 60

Build an alien

Make each of these shapes into an alien, using the stickers from the sticker pages.

Floating around

Astronauts do some of their training underwater because being in the water feels like floating in Space. Can you spot...

- six astronauts
- five safety divers
- a lost flipper

- three clouds of bubbles
- a red face mask
- a drill

Can you find four more badges like this one?

35

Fire...

Planet Fiera is covered with volcanoes, fire and boiling lava.
Help Zia to find a safe route back to her home.

Zia

Zia's home

...and ice

On planet Frozo, everyone lives in caves in the ice. Help Timo get to the Great Cave, stopping off to see Mota and Pim on the way.

Space tourists

One day, tourists may be able to fly into Space.

This tourist flight is due to leave, but someone is late. Draw a line to take her to the launch base, as quickly as you can. Try not to bump into the sides.

SPACE FLIGHT LAUNCH BASE

Are there enough helmets for each tourist to have one?

tourists ....
helmets ....

YES / NO

Everyone's on a spacecraft, ready to take off. Find the face stickers on the sticker pages and press one onto each window.

The spacecraft is far above Earth. Can you spot these countries, below the spacecraft?

Australia

Japan

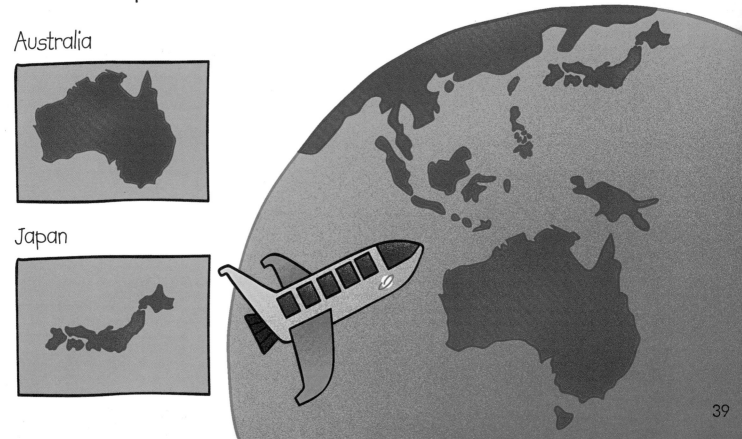

Draw a line to take the rocket around the red planet, past the yellow star, then to the green planet. How many white stars does it pass?

.... stars

Each rocket below is the same colour as the planet it's going to. Draw a line to link each rocket to its planet.

Follow the trails to find out where each rocket came from.

This rocket is heading back to Earth. It can only travel along lines that go through stars, but not through anything else.
Which way should it go?

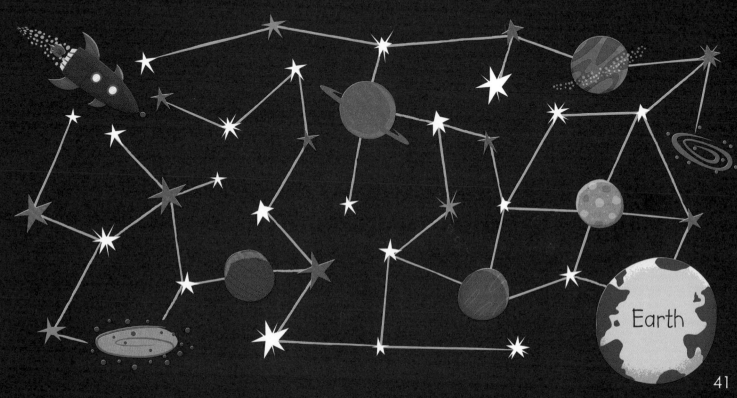

Earth

The Solar System

Earth is one of eight planets that travel around the Sun. The Sun and these planets are called the Solar System.

On these pages, there's a description of each planet. Find the sticker on the sticker pages that matches each description and press it on.

asteroid belt

MERCURY
Closest to the Sun and covered with craters

EARTH
Covered with sea and land

THE SUN

VENUS
Covered with thick clouds

MARS
Red, and smaller than Earth

SATURN
Has big rings of dust,
rocks and ice around it

JUPITER
Has a big red
spot on it

URANUS
Looks as if it's tilted,
with pale rings around it

NEPTUNE
Looks blue because
of gases around it

The spot is a huge
storm called the
Great Red Spot.

This is Pluto. It used to be called a planet,
but then scientists decided it was too small.

Alien spacecraft

Zip, Zap and Zop are flying around. Who came from each planet?

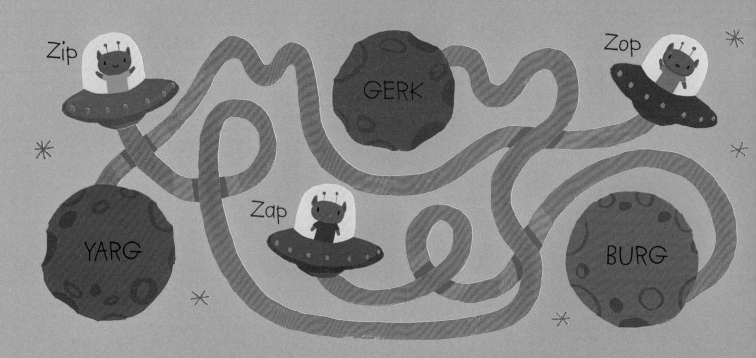

Draw more aliens in this flying saucer.

Add more lights, too.

Bogo, Bigi and Baga are going back to their planet. Who gets there first? Write the answer to the sum behind each spacecraft. The one with the highest number gets there first.

4 + 2 = ...   Bogo

5 – 3 = ...   Bigi

6 + 1 = ...   Baga

.... gets there first.

Draw more flying saucers in this space.

1. Draw an oval.

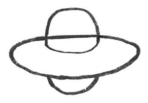

2. Add curves above and below it.

3. Add lights and an alien. Colour the flying saucer.

Space visitors

In the future, astronauts may travel to other planets.
On these pages, astronauts are exploring an imaginary planet.
Can you spot...

an astronaut
lifting a rock

an astronaut
in a crater

an astronaut
holding a flag

a space buggy
with a red roof

How many of each of these can you see?

purple rock ....   crater ....

volcano ....   pool of water ....

A long journey

This spacecraft has a long way to go. It needs to get to the space tunnel, which will take it to a distant part of Space...

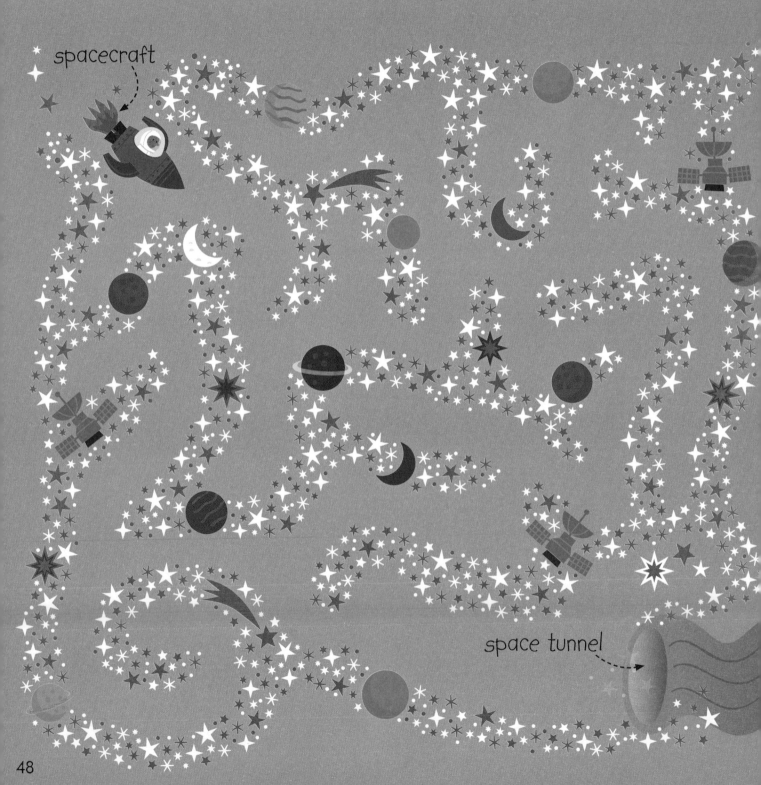

spacecraft

space tunnel

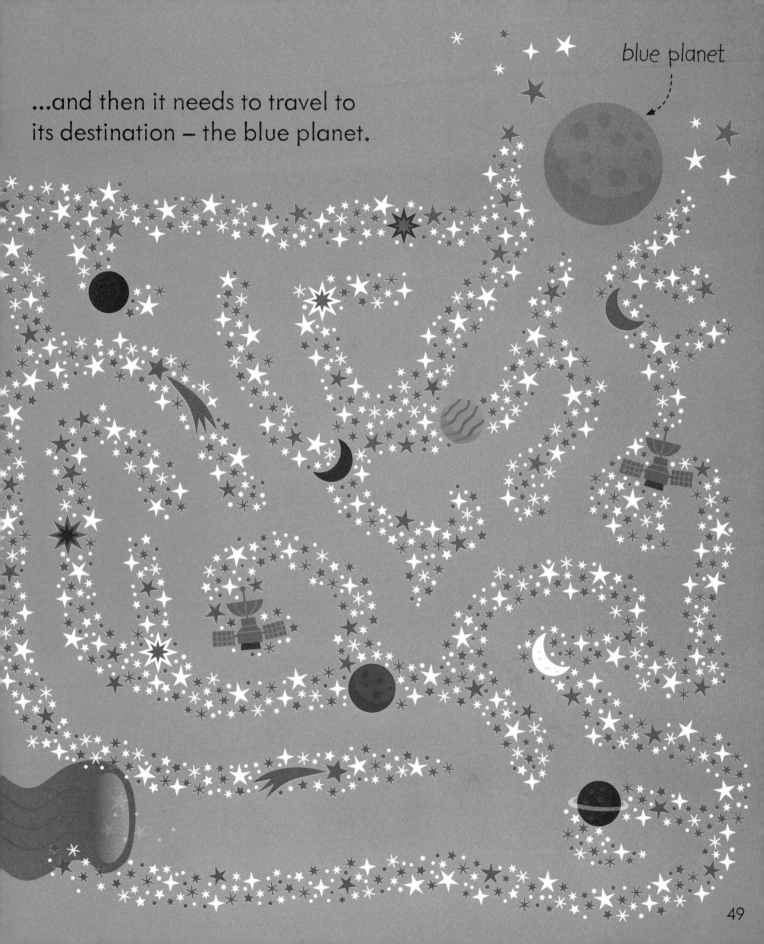

...and then it needs to travel to its destination – the blue planet.

blue planet

Alien planet

Two aliens are living on this planet, but there's room for lots more. Follow the steps to draw more aliens, then colour them.

How to draw an alien:

1. Draw a head and a body.

2. Add arms, legs and feelers.

3. Draw eyes, a nose and a mouth.

4. Colour the alien with bright colours.

Colour the stars, too.

You could use different colours for each alien.

51

Space museum

There are lots of amazing things to see in this Space museum. Which thing are most people looking at? Write the number of people above each one.

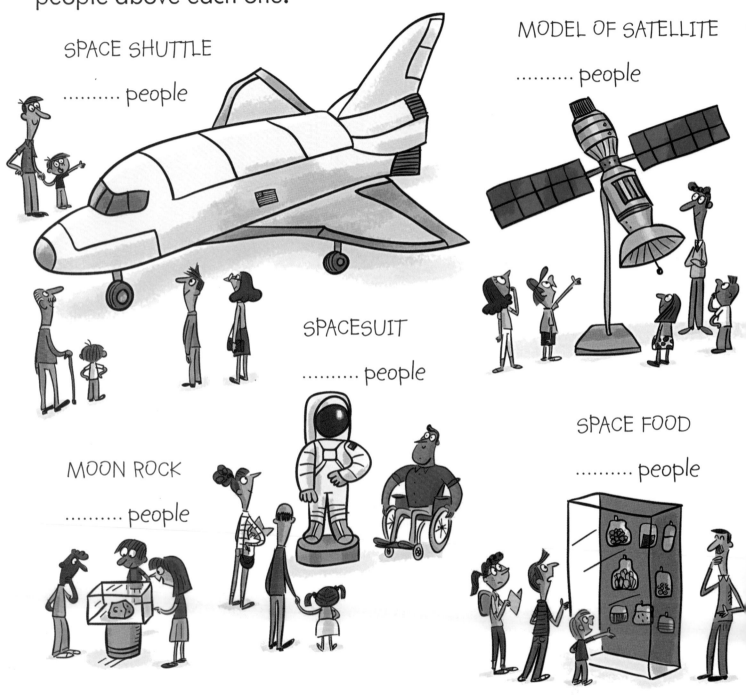

SPACE SHUTTLE

.... people

MODEL OF SATELLITE

.... people

SPACESUIT

.... people

MOON ROCK

.... people

SPACE FOOD

.... people

Most people are looking at the ....

Lucy wants to see the model of the moon buggy.
Which path should she take – A, B or C?

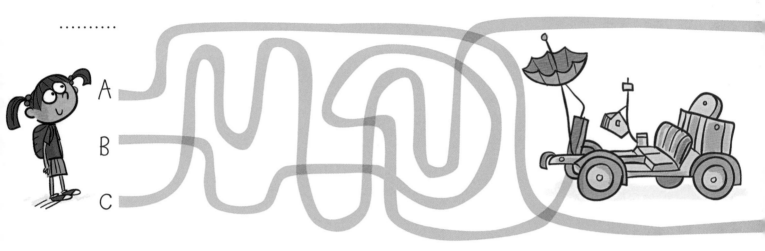

....

A

B

C

Meteorites are rocks that
fall to Earth from Space.
How many are there here?

....

Draw the other half of this
spacesuit used for spacewalks.

A base in Space

Space stations are built from lots of different parts. Complete this space station using the stickers from the sticker pages.

These astronauts are living in a space station.
Can you spot and colour...

...someone sleeping?

...someone looking out of a window?

...a guitar?

...two books?

...a pair of glasses?

...someone doing exercise?

Then, colour the rest of the picture.

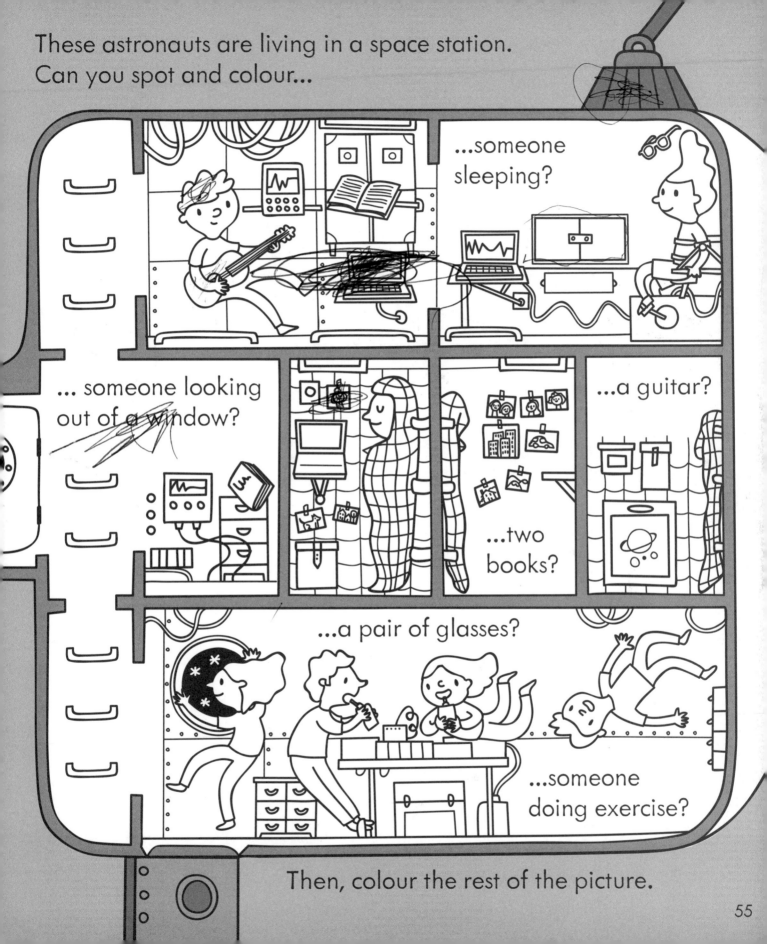

Stargazing

Some of the things below would help you to look at the stars. Draw a line to link each one to the correct word. Then, draw around the ones that would make it easier to see the stars.

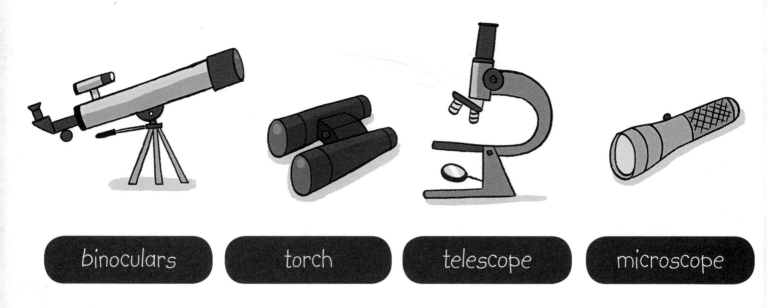

binoculars   torch   telescope   microscope

Constellations are arrangements of stars, like dot-to-dot puzzles. Starting with 1, link the numbers with lines to complete these two.

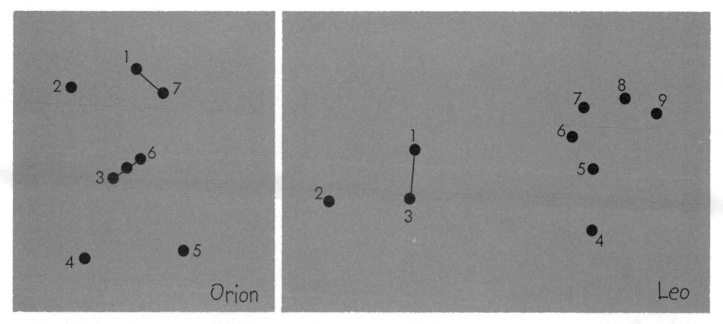

Orion

Leo

An astronomer is looking through her telescope. Which view can she see – A, B or C?

Galaxies are huge groups of stars, gathered together in different shapes. Which two galaxies below are exactly the same?

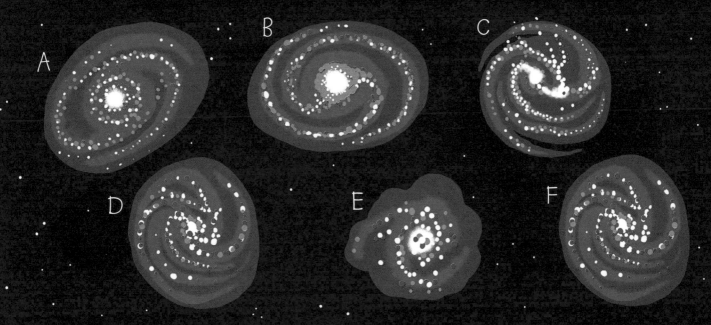

Lots of planets

Which planet is Zarko from? Read the clues to work it out:

- It's not the closest to the big star.
- It's not the smallest planet.
- It has rings around it.
- It isn't blue.

Zarko

big star

A planet is passing this faraway star.
But which planet is it – Eeby, Deeby, Beeby or Greeby?

Eeby

Deeby

Beeby

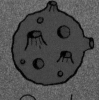

Greeby

Which of these planets has eight craters on it?
When you've spotted it, you could colour all the planets.

.... has eight craters on it.

Using the stickers on the sticker pages, add the Moon and lots of stars to this night sky.

Answers

2-3 What's out in Space?

- ○ stars
- ○ asteroids
- ○ pairs of stars

4-5 Astronauts

You should number the astronauts from left to right: 4, 2, 5, 1, 3

B is looking out of the window.

6-7 Mission Control

lights

- ○ pointing person
- ○ screen
- ○ map
- ○ clipboard
- ○ pencils
- ○ headphones
- ○ There are 5 mugs.

8-9 Lots of stars

There are 9 blue stars, 10 yellow stars and 8 red stars.

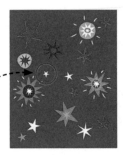

View C has an extra star.

12 Liftoff!

The missing numbers are 8, 5 and 2.

13 Back to Earth

Elias's suit is different. It is missing a button.

16-17 Working in Space

Noah – C
Minna – B
Adam – A

○ tool

You should number the plants from left to right: 3, 1, 2, 5, 4

Agnes has pedalled for 7 minutes, Max for 9 minutes, and Ivan for 8 minutes. Max has pedalled for longest.

18-19 Visiting the Moon

The astronaut has taken photo C.

No – the astronaut didn't make two of the footprints.

20-21 Astronaut training

They should build the camp at site C.

○ Ella   ○ Stan

24-25 Living in Space

One sock is missing.

running   driving car   having bath   walking dog

Lara – apple
Lucas – orange
Isabella – banana
Pierre – strawberry

The baby is missing from the screen.

26-27 Spacecraft

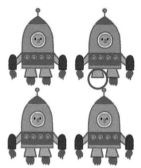 

28-29 Alien party

○ aliens with spots   ○ lots of arms
○ three eyes   ○ party hats
○ baby alien   ○ dancing aliens

30-31 The night sky

Yes, Eric and Lena can see everything in their book.

Square B completes the scene.

Martha can see 9 stars.

34-35 Floating around

- ○ astronauts
- ○ divers
- ○ lost flipper
- ○ bubbles
- ○ face mask
- ○ drill
- ○ badges

36-37 Fire... ...and ice

38-39 Space tourists

Yes, there are enough.
There are 5 tourists
and 5 helmets.

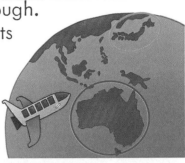

- ○ Australia
- ○ Japan

40-41 Busy rockets

○ The rocket passes 5 white stars.

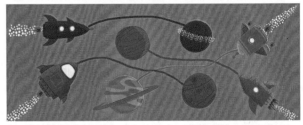

A = red planet, B = yellow planet,
C = blue planet

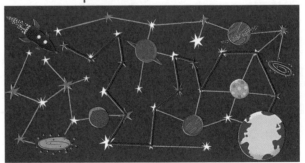

44-45 Alien spacecraft

Zip – Gerk, Zap – Burg, Zop – Yarg

Bogo: $4 + 2 = 6$, Bigi: $5 - 3 = 2$,
Baga: $6 + 1 = 7$. Baga gets there first.

46-47 Space visitors

- ○ astronaut lifting rock
- ○ astronaut in crater
- ○ astronaut holding flag
- ○ space buggy with red roof

5 ○
2 ○
4 ○
2 ○

48-49 A long journey

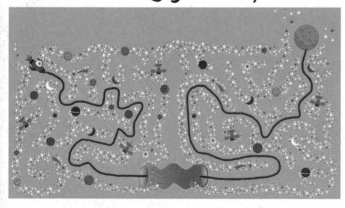

52-53 Space museum

Space Shuttle: 6 people, Model of satellite: 5 people, Spacesuit: 4 people, Moon rock: 3 people, Space food: 4 people. Most people are looking at the Space Shuttle.

Lucy should take path B.

There are 9 meteorites.

54-55 A base in Space

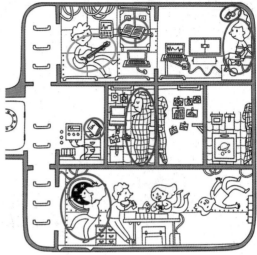

- ○ sleeping
- ○ looking out
- ○ books
- ○ guitar
- ○ glasses
- ○ doing exercise

56-57 Stargazing

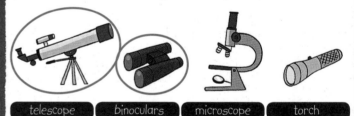

| telescope | binoculars | microscope | torch |

The astronomer can see view C.

Galaxies D and F are exactly the same.

58-59 Lots of planets

Zarko is from this planet.

Greeby is passing the star.

Planet D has eight craters on it.

First published in 2015 by Usborne Publishing Ltd., Usborne House, 83-85 Saffron Hill, London EC1N 8RT, England. www.usborne.com © 2015 Usborne Publishing Ltd.